The First Smile

By dar riddle

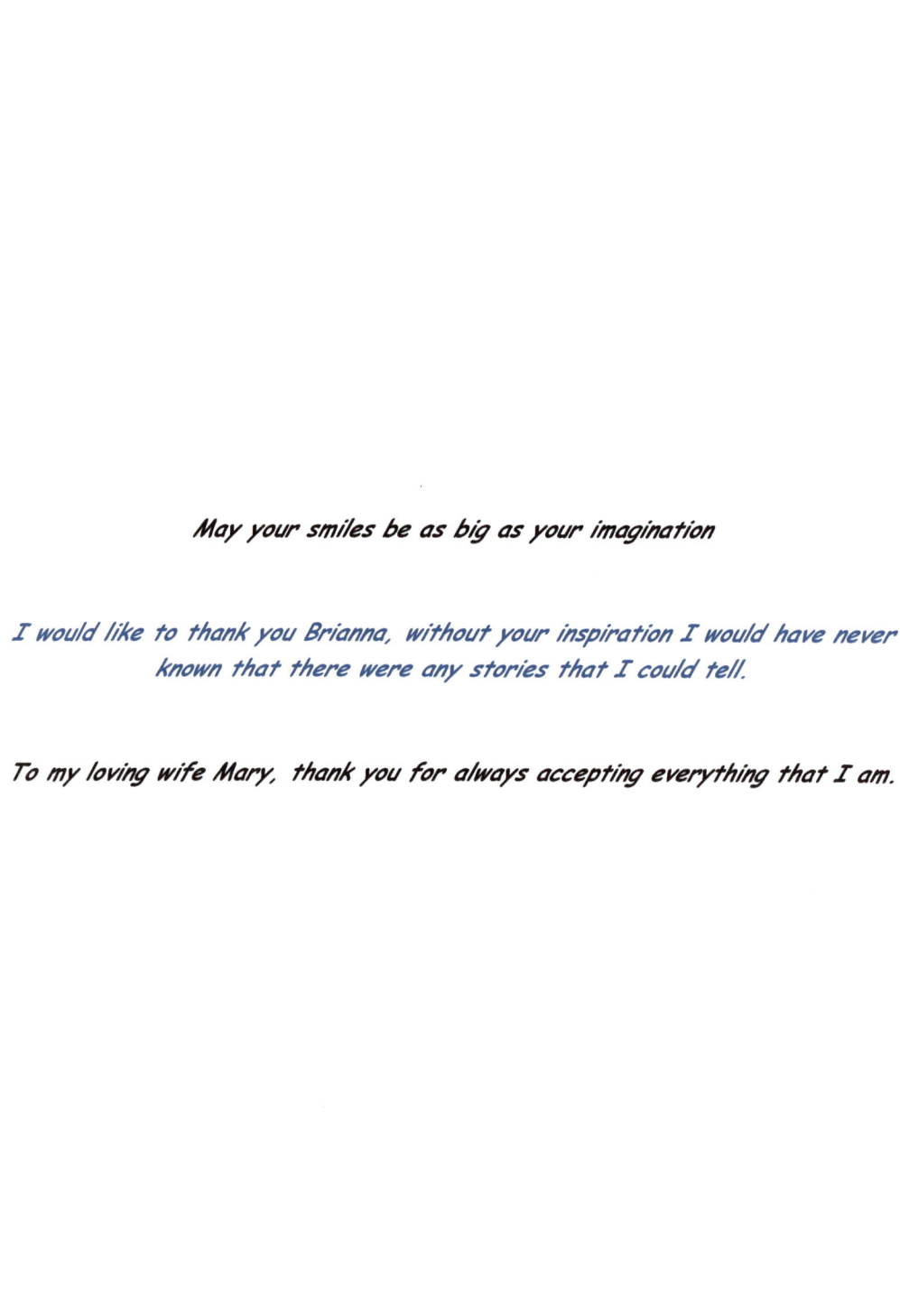

May your smiles be as big as your imagination

I would like to thank you Brianna, without your inspiration I would have never known that there were any stories that I could tell.

To my loving wife Mary, thank you for always accepting everything that I am.

About the author

Darnell p Riddle was born in Battle Creek Michigan in 1971 and currently resides in Middlebury Indiana. This is his first children's book in the Frownusville series. He is father, writer, poet, husband and friend.

"if you begin and end with a smile, what else do you need?"

Dar

The First Smile

the first smile

long ago and far way in a town called frownusville there lived two sisters, sadda and grimma. sadda was always bright and upbeat and grimma was always shiny and cheerful. they were twins who shared everything and agreed upon nothing. if sadda said, 'yes', then grimma said, 'no' and that was just the way it was.

now sadda and grimma lived in a time when the corners of everyone's mouths were always pointed down. if a person was in a bad kind of mood, the mouth was frowning. and if a person was as happy as happy can be, the mouth was still frowning. there was nothing wrong with this, it was normal, and it was the same all throughout frownusville. no one even noticed... no one except sadda and grimma that is.

you see, sadda was a dreamer, who dreamed of changing the world. she thought that one person could make a difference. so she decided to be that person.

now grimma didn't have big dreams, her greatest joy was topping her sister whenever she could. and she also decided to change the world, but better than sadda.

i am going to change the world better than my sister can change it

if sadda got an 'A' in school, then grimma got an 'A+'. if sadda went out and worked to make a dollar, then grimma would go and make two dollars. that was their life. always disagreeing and always out-doing each other. and of course always frowning, as everyone did in frownusville.

sadda and grimma were both very smart girls. sadda, when she had grown up, had decided to be an inventor. and grimma, when she too had grown up, decided to be a better inventor.

sadda moved to one side of frownusville and grimma moved to the other.
they both began to invent the most wondrous things. sadda invented hot and
grimma invented cold. sadda made sunshine and clouds while grimma made
raindrops and thunder.

on and on they went, making a magnificent this or a stupendous that until they
had invented most everything you could imagine.

they made lakes and mountains and fire and snowflakes and butterflies
and puppies and popcorn. you name it, they invented it. they even made a
something that does nothing and a nothing that does something...everyone
loved those.

they spent so much time over the years inventing stuff, that they
forgot to miss each other. so when they got older, they were alone and
separated from each other on opposite sides of frownusville. deep in their
hearts they really, truly missed each other... but they had invented loneliness
long ago.

one day, sadda decided that she wanted to live out the rest of her days
in the company of her sister grimma. she started to think of making her a gift
as a peace offering. grimma, feeling the same way, decided to make a better
peace offering.

so the two set themselves to thinking of what marvelous thing to give the other. they thought long and hard and could come up with nothing. they had invented everything. oh what a mess they were in. they couldn't possibly show up to make peace without a peace offering.

so they sat and they thought and then they thought some more. finally,
sadda had a splendtastic thought and grimma had a brightstanding one of her
own... 'i will take something i already made and make it even more superbly
fantastical', they each thought.

so sadda took the sunshine she had made long ago and made it even
more bright and warm and headed towards grimma's house. grimma took the
raindrops she invented and made them even more refreshing and cool and she
also set out for her sister's home.

on came sadda, sunshine in tow... on came grimma, raindrops close
behind. what a glorious sight it made. and whatever was going on had caught
the attention of the entire town and everyone came out to see what was what.

closer and closer the two sisters got, but neither had known how their gift would react with the other. all they knew was that they were going to see their sister with peace in their hearts.

well the two gifts mixed and mingled the closer they got. and the more the rain did rain the more the sunshine got hot. there was a blinding flashbam!

all shiny and wet and a tremendous whoompow! soaked with brightness.

so they looked to see what was what and they saw what they saw. a

'rainflower' , sadda wanted it named. look, 'it's a sunbow!', grimma
exclaimed.

the townsfolk got worried, they knew the sisters had never agreed upon anything. but to their surprise, the sisters agreed to call it a 'rainbow'...it was the first time the two had agreed on anything.

the sisters hugged each other with excitement, but when they did, they both lost control of their gifts and everything went wild. a wind started blowing and things began flipping and flying around. everything went crazy and it was too much for the sisters to handle.

even the rainbow had problems. it grew and grew and got knocked upside

down. then it exploded all over the town.

bits of upside-down rainbow flew here and flew there. everyone in town
was hit square in the mouth. and when they recovered and looked at their
faces, the frowns were all gone and smiles took their places.

and that's how sadda and grimma invented the smile... so each smile you see is a tiny rainbow turned upside-down, bursting with life and hiding a frown.

dar

www.ingramcontent.com/pod-product-compliance
Lightning Source LLC
Chambersburg PA
CBHW041033170626
46815CB00005B/300